# FaceSpace

# FaceSpace

## Adrian Chamberlain

*Orca currents*

ORCA BOOK PUBLISHERS

**Library and Archives Canada Cataloguing in Publication**

Chamberlain, Adrian, 1958-
FaceSpace / Adrian Chamberlain.
(Orca currents)

Issued also in electronic formats.
ISBN 978-1-4598-0151-6 (bound).--ISBN 978-1-4598-0150-9 (pbk.)

I. Title  II. Series: Orca currents
PS8605.H339F33 2013          jC813'.6          C2012-907297-4

First published in the United States, 2013
**Library of Congress Control Number:** 2012952471

**Summary:** Fourteen-year-old Danny invents a fictitious friend
in an effort to fit in at school.

MIX
Paper from
responsible sources
FSC® C016245
www.fsc.org

*Orca Book Publishers is dedicated to preserving the environment and has
printed this book on Forest Stewardship Council® certified paper.*

Orca Book Publishers gratefully acknowledges the support for its
publishing programs provided by the following agencies: the Government
of Canada through the Canada Book Fund and the Canada Council for the Arts,
and the Province of British Columbia through the BC Arts Council
and the Book Publishing Tax Credit.

Cover photography by iStockphoto.com

ORCA BOOK PUBLISHERS
PO Box 5626, Stn. B
Victoria, BC Canada
V8R 6S4

ORCA BOOK PUBLISHERS
PO Box 468
Custer, WA USA
98240-0468

www.orcabook.com
Printed and bound in Canada.

16 15 14 13 • 4 3 2 1

*For Penny and Katie.*

# Chapter One

Do you ever feel like everyone is having the best time of their lives but you? I've been getting that lately. And I mean a lot.

It's mostly FaceSpace. Like everyone else, I've been on FaceSpace for a while. Seems like everyone's having fun.

Not me.

Take today. Sunday morning. My brother Scott is home from college for the weekend. What he's doing this very second is sleeping. Even though it's, like, almost noon.

There are two beds in our room, and Scott is stretched out on his. He's really tall—like, six foot three. And I hate to admit it, but he's a super handsome guy. He's the sort of guy who attracts girls like Häagen-Dazs attracts flies, with absolutely no effort on his part.

That kills me. *Absolutely no effort.*

You know why Scott's still sleeping? Because he was out partying last night. Partying like a rock star. He came home at 2:34 AM. I know, because he woke me up when he stumbled in.

I fire up the computer while Scott snores away. I check out my FaceSpace page. I have fifty-three friends. Not too shabby, I guess, although most people have way more. Like my friend Brad. He's a point guard on the Oak Bay Invaders, the best ball handler on the team. The best *basketball* handler, is what I mean.

Brad has 763 friends. Seven. Hundred. And sixty-three. And he doesn't even care about FaceSpace. He hardly ever goes on it. I know, because we're best friends. We've known each other since we were eight.

Today there are all these status updates on FaceSpace about what everybody did last night. It was Saturday night, so everyone was partying, having a good time. My feed is full of things like "Hey, dude, we took it to the limit last night," and "Hey, Donny, did you guys ever find B-Tone?" and "There must have been 100 people at that raver last night." A hundred people, eh? Why didn't anyone invite me? That's what I'd like to know.

You know what I did last night? I played Parcheesi with my mom. My mom is crazy about Parcheesi.

If word got out that I played Parcheesi with my mother on a Saturday night, my name would be mud at school. Or make that dork. Not that I have that cool a reputation anyway.

Scott rolls over in his bed and moans. He's still wearing his clothes from last night, for God's sake. He sits up and rubs his eyes.

"Headache?" I say, all helpful-like.

He rubs his eyes again and shakes his head.

"Holy man," he says.

"Good party? Enjoyable?"

"Ummm," Scott says. "Yeah. Great party. Great, great party. So what did you get up to last night, Danny?"

"Not much," I say. "Hung out with Mom."

"Mmmm," says Scott. "I feel wretched."

He shoves his hand into his pants and scratches himself, then wanders into the bathroom. There's this splashy sound of Scott taking a great big whiz. He doesn't even close the door. Classy. Then I hear the scratch of a match and smell cigarette smoke. Even though cigarettes are outlawed in our house.

This is my life. Playing Parcheesi with Mom and listening to my brother take a leak.

I turn back to the computer. I'm really into architecture, designing buildings and stuff. That's what I'd like to do for real one day.

Right now I'm designing a super deluxe house. It's the kind of house a hip-hop star would have. For one thing, there's, like, this huge recording studio in it. It's the size of a barn. The studio has a bar, a pool-table room and its own gym.

It has nine bedrooms and an infinity pool, one of those pools with the edge that looks like it goes on forever, right into the horizon. There's an entertainment theater with a flat-screen TV the size of a movie-theater screen. Pretty cool, eh?

I've got this 3-D design program for designing your own house or building or whatever. You can even walk in, using your computer, and take a tour. I can work on this stuff for hours. Time flies by. I'll start working on something at eleven in the morning, and then before I know it, it's, like, five o'clock or something. And I'm starving because I didn't have lunch.

"What's that, little bro?"

Scotty is standing behind me, puffing on his cigarette. I didn't even know he was there. He scratches the bristle on his handsome, movie-actor's chin. Scotty has a real good beard. He could grow a full beard in four days. Not me. I have about five hairs on my chin.

"Nothing," I say. My architect stuff is kind of private.

"What's that?" says Scott. He points to the rock-star recording studio.

"Recording studio," I say.

"Cool," says Scotty, yawning. He goes into the bathroom and flicks his cigarette into the toilet, which makes a hiss. "Well, I'm gonna take a shower. I'm meeting Jill."

Jill is Scotty's girlfriend. Or rather, his old girlfriend. He's got another girl-friend at college. Only Jill doesn't know that yet.

Where's my girlfriend? That's what I'd like to know. I'm fourteen years old and have never even had a girlfriend. That's, like, a crime or something.

I go to my FaceSpace page to see if there are any messages for me. Nope. There is an update from Brad though. Last night he wrote, "Heading out with J-J and the boys." And underneath, there are about twenty-five responses.

"Atta boy, Brad." "Don't party too hard, big guy."

I message Brad. "Hey, man, wanna hang out this aft?" Maybe we can go to the mall or whatever. Anything would be good.

Then my cell goes off.

"Hey, buddy." It's Brad.

"Hey. I just messaged you."

"Yeah, I know. I can't hang today, man."

"How come?" I say.

"Basketball practice. An extra one. We've got finals coming up, remember? Coach says we need to practice from, like, one to four."

"Maybe after then," I say.

"Sorry, Dan-o. I've got homework after. Math is killing me."

"Okay. See ya," I say.

The front door slams. That'll be Scotty, heading out. Jeez, what am I gonna do today? Just to pass the time,

I check out Brad's FaceSpace page. It's mostly pictures of him playing basketball. There's one of him sinking a slam dunk. Nice shot. I think I was at that game. Oak Bay versus Nanaimo. Fifty-two to thirty-six. I have a good memory for useless stuff.

There are lots of pictures, for sure. Here's one of Brad at a party or something. Everyone is sitting on a couch. He's with some girl. What's her name? I forget.

I suddenly feel lousy. I throw myself onto my bed like a sack of potatoes, lie on my back and stare at the ceiling. There's this poster on the ceiling that's been up there since I was eight. It's actually a map that shows all the constellations— all the galaxies and all that. For some reason, this map bugs me. I reach up, rip it down and crumple it into a ball. Stupid map. Yikes. My hands are all dusty now.

Then I remember I'm supposed to go clothes shopping this afternoon with Mom. Crap. How boring. Step right up, ladies and gentlemen. Welcome to the exciting, super thrilling, action-packed life of Danny McBride.

# Chapter Two

I hear a car starting up outside. I roll off the bed and look out the bedroom window in time to see Scott take off to visit Jill. Scott's got a great car. It's an old Alfa Romeo convertible. Black. Practically no one else has one. He got it cheap and fixed it up. The muffler makes a low rumble each time he switches gears. It's pretty cool.

I have homework to do, but I'm not in the mood. I do okay in school. I get mostly Bs and some As. I pick up a wooden ruler with my teeth and poke the pile of textbooks on my desk with it. Then I start singing "Iron Man" by Black Sabbath.

*Has he lost his mind?*
*Can he see or is he blind?*

Can he see or is he blind! That kills me. I like old rock. The Rolling Stones, the Beatles. And Black Sabbath. Most kids my age aren't into this stuff.

I keep jabbing my books with the ruler and singing those two lines over and over in this crazy Ozzy-with-a-ruler-between-his-teeth voice.

Then Mom calls me to go to the mall to buy new clothes. I hate this. I'm not much of a style guy. When it comes to fashion, it's hard to figure out what's going on.

What's cool? What's sorta cool? What's definitely not cool and to be avoided no matter what?

One store at the mall has some great clothes. I guess they are hip-hop fashions. But I could never pull this off. If I wore this stuff to school, guys would be saying, "McBride, you poser." Or, "Look at McBride. What a knob." That sort of thing.

Instead, I let Mom pick the blandest type of clothes. I guess I seem bored, because after an hour, she hands me thirty bucks and tells me to go buy myself something.

She probably wants me to get lost so she can shop for herself. No problem, Mom, thirty bucks is thirty bucks. I go into the CD store, which is really mostly a DVD store. I start riffling through a rack of bargain discs. I find *Doolittle*, by the Pixies. The Pixies are an old-school band from the 1980s. They influenced Nirvana. The singer, a big chubby guy called Black Francis, sings in this strange voice, like he's a drowning cat or something. They're a really good band.

I've already downloaded most of the Pixies' music, but I decide to buy the album for the artwork and all. When I turn around, *Doolittle* in hand, guess who's there in the store? Megan.

Megan is in some of my classes. I kind of like her. I've talked to her exactly three times. Here's a transcript of our conversations:

Me (in English): Hey there. Um, do you have a pen I can borrow?
Megan: I think so. Here ya go.

Me (in Socials): Did he say Ecuador is bordered by Peru?
Megan: Um, I'm not sure.

Me (in Math): Man, this is hard, eh?
Megan: You're not kidding.

It's hard to tell if a girl likes you from this. Sometimes I think about these three conversations. If I'm in a good mood, I think, Yeah, Megan totally likes me. If I'm in a bad mood, I think, Danny, you are a loser and Megan thinks you suck badly.

So there I am, face-to-face with Megan for real. She's smiling. She's got blond hair, green eyes and funny teeth— kind of like buckteeth, but super cute.

"Hi," she says. "Hey, I know you. From English."

"Oh yeah," I say. Smooth, right?

"So…What you got there?" she asks.

"What?" I'm so freaked about seeing Megan, I totally forget what's in my hands.

"What did you buy?" she says.

"Um. *Doolittle*. It's by that band the Pixies. You know it?"

"No."

"Well, they're a really good band. You know Nirvana? Like, Nirvana with Kurt Cobain? Well, they were influenced by the Pixies. All that loud, soft, loud stuff? That was the Pixies' idea. Their singer, Black Francis—he's the best singer in rock. He screams like no one else. And their bassist, Kim Deal—when she wasn't in the Pixies, she was in the Breeders, who are a totally great band too. You know that song 'Cannonball'? Well, that was the Breeders. Anyway, *Doolittle* is a great album. Maybe the best album ever. It's totally, totally, totally cool."

Megan smiles again and says, "Okay. Well, see ya in class then."

I stand there with my album in my sweaty hand and watch her walk away. And I think, Oh man, did you babble like an idiot for a full minute? Jeez.

Mom and I meet up, and we drive home. I've got my new clothes and my new album, but I'm not feeling that great, to tell the truth. Seeing Megan like that bummed me out. I keep thinking of stuff I should have said.

Me: Hey there, Megan.
Megan: Hey there. What's in the bag?
Me: Doolittle. The Pixies. They're the greatest band on earth. Wanna go listen to it?
Megan: Sure. Thanks, Danny.

Or:

Me: Hey there, Megan.
Megan: Hi.
Me: I know you from English. You may be the best-looking girl in that class. And believe me, there's a lot of good-looking girls in that class.
Megan: Hey, thanks.
Me: Wanna go out sometime?
Megan: Yes.

Or:

Me: Hey, babe.
Megan: Hey.
Me: I'll let you hang with me, if you like.
Megan: Is that the *Doolittle* album? You must be cool. Okay, sure.
Me: Cool is my middle name. Let's roll.

Yeah, I know. That last one is pretty stupid.

Sometimes imagining stuff like this makes me feel better. Not today. Today I keep reliving what really happened with Megan, and then I feel bad. I wish I was better at talking to girls. It would be good if they had a class for that that was taught by some righteous guy, a James Bond kind of guy. He would teach you how to act, what to say. Then you'd know what to do. Of course, a class like that would have to be top secret. What if people found out you were enrolled? That would be social suicide.

When we get back to the house, Mom asks if I want to model my new clothes. I tell her I'm not in the mood. Instead, I go to my room and start working on Lego City.

For about six months, I've been building an entire city from Lego. I put it on a huge plywood board that I keep hidden under my bed. Yes, I know this may seem a little dorky. But it's also interesting. I'm building a city of the future. It's on two levels. All the cars and buses are on the lower level. The top level is just for pedestrians, so that people can walk around like normal human beings without getting run over. And there will be parks in the middle of the city, markets, playgrounds—whatever.

When I'm working on Lego City, I forget about the time, like I'm living in that make-believe world. The part I'm working on now is a huge aquarium in the middle of the park.

I'm wondering whether Lego makes parts for dolphins when the door opens.

"Mom says it's dinnertime. Hey, what's that?" Scott stands there, hands in his jean pockets, grinning. I shove Lego City back under my bed real fast—too fast, because part of a skyscraper breaks off and rolls across the floor. Scott picks it up.

"What's this?" he says. "Hey, is this Lego?"

"No," I say.

"It is Lego."

"No it's not."

"Isn't that for kids?" asks Scott.

"Shut up, Scott. Just hand it over."

He chuckles and gives me the skyscraper. Then Scott kneels to look at Lego City, pulling it out from under the bed.

"Danny," he says, "this is sort of amazing. But it's also pretty weird."

"It's not weird," I say.

"It wouldn't be if you were nine years old. Lego is for kids. Anyway, you better come to dinner. Mom made ribs."

I throw the piece of the Lego skyscraper at Scott's big fat head. But he's already gone. Instead, it hits the door and breaks into pieces.

Man, am I mad. Not just about Scott, but everything. Talking to Megan. Not being able to hang out with Brad today. I slam Lego City under my bed, not even caring about the chunks that break off and roll on the floor. I stick the *Doolittle* album in the stereo and crank up the volume. The first cut is "Debaser." Black Francis is singing all crazy, screaming about cutting up eyeballs and "girlie so groovy" and being a debaser. I'm not sure what it all means, but it suits the way I feel right now. It's like I want to break out of my situation. The whole thing—school, living at home, not having a girlfriend. I'd like to be, I don't know. Someone else. Not me.

Scott is calling me again for dinner, but it's hard to hear above the smash-crash-bang of the drums, guitars and crazy Black Francis.

This is when it all starts. This very second, with "Debaser" blaring on the stereo, Lego strewn all over the floor and the smell of Mom's ribs wafting down the hall.

If I could take it all back, would I? You bet. But sometimes we do stuff we regret, almost without thinking. It's like something takes over. You know what I mean?

# Chapter Three

On Sunday night I'm still mad at Brad for not hanging out. I go onto Brad's FaceSpace site and start checking out his photos. There's one of Brad posing with Grant, this really tall guy on the basketball team. They're both smiling, each holding a basketball. Grant is a total knob with bright red hair. I dislike him, to tell the truth. Once I saw Grant in the hallway doing this super spastic imitation of the way I walk. The more I think about it, Grant is a total jerk.

Then I get a great idea. I have a computer program for altering photos. I download Brad's photo and start messing around with it. Instead of smiling, he's biting his lower lip, like he's worried or something. The effect is totally comical. I change his eyes, so that instead of being normal-sized, they're really, really small. I expand Grant's head until it's about the size of a pumpkin.

This cracks me up. It looks so funny, I almost fall off my chair. I also have a little program that allows me to post on FaceSpace anonymously. I post the picture on Brad's page.

And then I really get into it. I mess around with four or five of Brad's photos. There's one of him standing, arms linked with his mom and dad, in front of some restaurant. I alter that one so Brad's eyes are rolling like he's bored or something. Classic.

When I'm done, the clock says it's one thirty in the morning. I fall into bed, still wearing my clothes. Scott's already asleep. I didn't even notice him come into the room.

The next morning when the alarm buzzes, I feel terrible. Today is my worst day of the week, schoolwise. I have math, science and socials. I hate science. Who wants to play with dead frogs?

At lunchtime, I walk to the table in the corner where Brad and I always sit. Brad is already there.

"Hey, pal," I say, plunking myself down. In my lunch bag I find a jam sandwich. I think it's strawberry jam. What the heck? Does Mom think I'm eight years old?

"Hey yourself," says Brad.

"What's up? You don't look like your usual bright-eyed self," I say.

"Ah, nothing. Do you know someone was playing around with my photos? On FaceSpace."

I put down my jam sandwich. Holy crap. I'd forgotten about that. I get a weird feeling along my spine, like the hairs are standing up.

"Really?" I say. "You don't say."

"Yeah," says Brad. "Here, check it out on my phone. Just a sec. Okay. See? Look at that."

He shows the one of him and giant-headed Grant. It's the one where Brad's got tiny little eyes and is biting his lip. It looks so crazy funny that I can't help laughing a little.

"Hey, man, don't laugh. This is serious," Brad says.

"Well, at least Grant looks normal," I say.

"Danny. I'm serious. I'd like to kill whoever did this."

"Hmm," I say. "Well, maybe I can help you track him down. Or, um, her. Could be a girl."

"Yeah?"

"There might be a way to find out. I'm good with this kind of thing."

Brad smiles, his face lighting up. He's really a good guy. Now I feel bad. Who does this to a friend?

"Don't worry, bud," I say. "We can catch this dude. And if we do, we should totally get revenge."

I start to get a different kind of feeling. I imagine a creepy hacker guy doing a number on my good friend Brad—some old dude with a wrinkled face. In my mind, he's totally bald, except for a few hairs on top of his head. What a jerk. Are we going to stand for this? No way. This guy is going down. I tell Brad that if we catch whoever changed his photos, we should confront him.

After a minute or two of me yakking away, Brad gives me a funny look.

"Danny. Calm down. It's not that big a deal," he says.

Brad asks if I want to watch him at basketball practice after school. I say okay. Not that I'm crazy about basketball, but it's something to do. My homework is really piling up, but I can put it off for an hour. To tell the truth, I'm happy that Brad asked me to come along.

The whole team is shooting baskets. The Oak Bay Invaders. They wear red uniforms with a picture of a horse on the front. The *I* in Invaders looks like a horn coming out of the horse's head. They look more like the Oak Bay Unicorns.

I'm sitting high in the bleachers, minding my own business, when Megan walks into the gym. Right away, I feel my face getting hot. I remember our last conversation at the record store. Man, that was embarrassing, me blabbing away like that. I wonder if I should pretend I don't notice her.

Before I can think of what to do, Megan climbs the bleachers and plops down beside me.

"Hey there!" she says with a smile.

"Uh, hi," I say.

"I didn't know you were a basketball fan. I thought you were more of a music guy."

I tell her I'm only watching because Brad's my buddy. It turns out Megan is a friend of Brad's too. The conversation is awkward at first, mostly because I feel shy. But Megan is so friendly, I start to feel comfortable right away, and soon we're chatting away like old pals. Imagine. Danny McBride shooting the breeze with a great-looking girl like Megan.

And is she running away? Is she rushing out of the gym, screaming? No, she is not. This is good—fantastic even.

After half an hour, I tell Megan I'd better head home because of all my homework. She decides to cut out too, so we walk together through the school hallways toward my locker.

We're almost there when a gang of kids walking the other way says hi to Megan. Then one of them, this big guy, gives me a shove. For no reason. I stumble and bang into a locker, but luckily I don't fall down or anything. I don't even know this guy. He's one of those wide-necked jerks who looks like a football player.

"What...?" I say.

They all laugh and keep walking down the hall, although a couple of the girls look away.

"Danny, are you okay?" asks Megan. She's actually concerned. Megan tells me the wide-necked guy used to like her. She never dated him or anything. Maybe he's jealous? Who knows? Now I feel awkward, like at the record shop. It's as if I'm ashamed or something, even though it wasn't my fault. My face is all hot again.

We say goodbye, and I trudge home. I go into my bedroom to tackle my homework. There's a ton of math. It takes two hours to get it done. I can't believe how much homework they give us. It makes me mad.

Then I remember the photos of Brad's that are still on my computer. I think maybe I should return them to normal and repost them as a kind of apology. But I don't fix them. No, instead, I make them worse. I give big-headed Grant two huge snaggle-teeth. I enlarge Brad's tiny eyes and make them all bloodshot. He now looks like a crazy space alien.

As I post the new photo on his page, I wonder why I am doing this. Brad hasn't done anything to me. It's going to bug him, big-time.

I check out my FaceSpace profile. There's a friend request from Megan. Fantastic. Cool. I accept that one fast. Maybe Megan doesn't think I'm a doob after all, despite what happened in the hall today.

If only I could be, I don't know, someone else. Someone who's always cool, who always knows what to do and say, someone popular.

I go onto a photo site and find a picture of a cool-looking guy. He looks like Tom Cruise as a teenager. I take the photo and create a fake FaceSpace profile. I call him James Bradbury. Then I get James to "friend" me on FaceSpace. There. One cool new friend.

The clock says 10:28 PM. I'm exhausted. I feel like I've run a marathon.

Not that I've ever run one. Not even close. I listen to some Pixies on my iPod, lying on my bed. I feel strange and unsettled.

After a while the feeling goes away, and I fall asleep.

# Chapter Four

At lunchtime Brad complains about someone making the photos on his FaceSpace page look worse.

"Who would do that?" he says, taking a big bite out of his meatball sandwich. It's a good-looking sandwich. Me, I've got jam again.

"Hmm," I said, reaching for an apple. "That's strange. And how were the pictures different? Like, how were they altered?"

"I don't know. My eyes were made way bigger in this one photo. It makes me look crazy. Maybe I should just delete them all," says Brad.

"No! I mean, no, Brad. That's a bad idea. Leave it for now. It'll help me track down the perpetrator."

"The perps," Brad says.

"Huh?"

"The perps. That's what they call them on TV. The bad guys."

"Right," I say. "The perps."

Just then Megan comes by. She says hi and asks if she can sit with us. We say sure. On her tray, she's got one carton of milk, an apple and a banana. That's all. Girls. Go figure.

We talk about Brad's basketball team. He says they're looking for a manager. Brad says I should apply for the position.

I shrug. "Nah. If anything, I'd rather be a player," I say. "But that would never happen. I'm no good at basketball."

"Well, think about the manager thing," says Brad.

"Why?"

"For starters, you get to travel with the team. We're likely going to Vancouver for the finals in a few months. It'll be a total blast."

"Danny, you should do it," says Megan.

"I dunno. I'll think about it."

We talk about classes. Megan says she's having trouble in math. She's good at English and art, but not math and science. This makes me happy. The math thing, that is. Because I'm pretty good at math. Maybe I can offer to help Megan with her homework. It's on the tip of my tongue to offer, but I can't quite say it. What if she says no?

I wish I could just come out with it, real casual. Something like:

Me: "Hey, Megan. You need help with your math. I can help."
Megan: "Golly, what a nice offer, Danny."
Me: "It's totally my pleasure."

Or:

Me: "Hey, Megs. Need help with the ol'fractions, integers and so forth? Danny boy to the rescue. Just say the word."
Megan: "Oh, Danny! You are so smart and generous. Perhaps later we can go to a movie."
Me: "Play your cards right, Megster, and that may very well just happen."

Ha. Dream on. I say nothing, of course. I am tongue-tied, as usual. In fact, my tongue feels weird and dry now. Like a dried-out sausage. I grab my water bottle and take a gulp.

And then Megan says, "Hey, Danny, who's this James guy on FaceSpace?"

I almost spit out my water. Man, that took me by surprise. James. What had I put on that fake profile anyway? Was it open to the public? Uh-oh.

"James," I say, real casual. "Oh yes. James Bradbury. Yeah. He's just moved to Canada. He's an old friend."

"What? I've never heard of him," says Brad.

"Well, you don't know everyone I know," I say. "James is from, uh, England. He's a family friend."

Just then a pop can sails over my head. Right out of the blue. It misses my right ear by, like, five inches. There's a muffled laugh from the other side of the cafeteria. What a zoo.

"Wow, England. Cool," says Megan. She politely doesn't mention my nearly getting nailed by a pop can.

So we start talking about James. Of course, I've got to make stuff up as I go along. James is from London. He and his family live in Vancouver, not here in Victoria. He plays bass in a punk-rock band. He drives an old Jaguar. It's the family car they shipped from England. I'm going on and on, hoping I don't make any mistakes. Megan and Brad keep asking questions. Every time they shoot one out, I'm dodging it like a bullet. Luckily, I'm fast on my feet.

"I notice he doesn't have any friends on FaceSpace," says Megan. "Except for you."

"Yeah. Well, that's because he's brand-new to Canada."

"Didn't he use FaceSpace in England?" Brad asks.

"Nope. Didn't have time. Too busy, um, playing bass in his punk band," I say.

Finally, Megan and Brad get off the subject of James. Thank God. I'm not sure how much longer I could have kept this up. My tongue is all dry again, so I take another big slug of water. Then I say bye and head off to my next class.

After school, there's a black sports car in our driveway. Big brother is back for another visit. When I get in the bedroom, Scott is sprawled on his bed, reading a textbook called *Introduction to Abnormal Psychology*.

"Hello, little bro," he says, grinning.

"Ah. Hi," I say.

What I really want to do right now is work on James Bradbury's FaceSpace profile. I need to make sure it fits all the made-up stuff I told Brad and Megan at lunch. I can't do it while Scott is in the room. Scott is the sort of guy who will ask what I'm doing. And then he'll spill the beans to everyone.

"Here for another visit?" I say, glancing over at my computer.

"Too noisy at our house. They're planning a kegger. I need to hit the books big-time. Get some major reading done."

"Really?" Scott shares a house with this bunch of frat guys. They are real boneheads. All they do is party.

"Yup. Really."

I wish Scott would buzz off. I keep looking at my computer and then back to Scott. I feel all hyper. Why doesn't Scott get lost so I can fix James's profile? I fold my arms and then unfold them. I fold them again. I look around the room, trying to look anywhere but at my computer.

"Hey, Danny, you seem uptight. You okay?" asks Scott. "Let me see if I can figure out your problem. It'll probably say what's wrong with you in my psych text."

He pretends to search his book, flicking one page after another.

"Okay. Let's see here. Anxiety. Possible hysteria."

"Scott, get lost. I need to use my computer."

"Ah. Irritability. Possible mental confusion."

I grab the pillow off my bed and peg it at Scott's head. He laughs and goes upstairs.

I sit at the computer and open James Bradbury's profile. Let's see. I write that he's from London. Under *Hobbies*, I write that he plays bass and likes punk music. I find a picture of an old Jaguar sedan. It is British racing green. I post it in his photos. That's the family car—great.

At suppertime, Scott goes on about college. Mostly he talks about his roommates. They all have goofy nicknames.

There is Pongo. The Sheik. I forget the others' names.

After supper, I zip downstairs again and add finishing touches to James's profile. I Photoshop a picture of him and me together. It's really a picture Mom took of me and Scott last summer, when we went to Butchart Gardens. I pull out Scott's face and replace it with James's. The lighting looks funny, so I adjust the shading. Then I resize it, and after that the photo looks pretty convincing. There's me and James, arms around each other, smiling away, with a whole bunch of flowers in the background.

Then, because I'm so pleased with myself, I take a chance. I put in a friend request from James to Megan. One click of the mouse, and it's done. She accepts about fifteen seconds later! How cool is that?

It's like James Bradbury is a real person or something. And I, Danny McBride, am his creator. Bwahaha. Maybe Scott's right. Maybe I do have some mental confusion. I decide to call it a night.

## Chapter Five

I'm having a very weird dream. I'm in the jungle in Vietnam—or at least, it seems like Vietnam. I've never even been there before. There are lots of bushes, and I've been captured by soldiers.

The soldiers are dressed in green combat uniforms, like in the movies. They have tied me to a tree, using thick rope. It's all rough and itchy. They are asking me questions about something bad that I've done. There is something about a false identity. They treat me like I'm a spy. I don't know what they're talking about. Because these soldiers are not getting the answers they want from me, they decide to cut off one of my legs. The biggest soldier, a mean-looking guy with a greasy black beard and squinty eyes, pulls out this massive chainsaw. He fires it up and gets closer, and closer, and—

"Ahhhhh!" I yell, bolting up like a jack-in-the-box. I'm completely disoriented.

That was super, super scary. I look over at Scott, who is snoring away in the next bed. That's it. That's the chainsaw noise. Scott needs to get one of these things you put on your nose at night to stop the snoring. This is getting out of hand.

"Scott!" I yell. I throw my pillow at his head. No response. He's a heavy sleeper.

Before I start to get ready for school, I sit down at the computer. I wonder if anyone's noticed the new details I added to James's profile last night.

James has fifty new friend requests already. Yes, that's right. Fifty people. They are all kids from my school. I guess they saw that Megan friended James. And because Megan's popular—and James seems cool—they want to be his friend too.

So James—I mean, me—accepts them all. But you know, it burns me. Some of these guys are people I tried to friend on my own profile. And they ignored me. Now some cool, handsome dude from the UK shows up, someone they don't even know, and they're all over him. It goes to show how shallow some people are.

I click away—accept, accept, accept. James will have more friends than me soon. I'm a little bit scared. There's no turning back now. James is out in the real world. And although he's fake, he's going to be interacting with real people, even if it is only on a computer.

Could this all backfire? I wonder. It could. What if I get found out? The thought causes a knot of fear to build in the bottom of my belly.

There's another terrific snore, more like a snort. Scott finally sits up. He is dazed, like he's come out of a hundred-year sleep.

"Snore much?" I say.

"What?" says Scott. He looks at me blankly.

"You were snoring. In fact, you snored so much, you gave me a nightmare."

"You're crazy," says Scott. "I never snore."

That morning at school, something is different. Something has happened. I'm walking down the hall as usual, with my backpack filled with twenty pounds of books. But now, every once in awhile, someone asks me about James.

It's, like, "Hey, Danny? Who's this new James guy?" Or, "Danny? Hey there, buddy. How do you know the English guy?"

To tell the truth, I do enjoy the attention. Sometimes I walk down the hall at school and feel like I'm invisible, like I don't even exist. It's a big school. There are so many kids here, you can get swallowed in the crowd. Now I'm somebody. Maybe somebody important even.

Today everything is a little shinier, a little brighter. The crummy gray lockers look, well, less crummy. The boring teachers seem less boring, even Mr. Cromwell, who wears a bow tie and drones on about the periodic table. The kids who sometimes get on my nerves are less irritating. That girl who sits in the front desk in socials and sticks up her hand every five minutes to answer a question doesn't bother me at all today.

Toward the end of the day, I'm getting excited. Maybe some of James's new friends are talking to him online. I can't wait to get home and see.

I fire up FaceSpace and see that there has been a flurry of James action. All the kids are asking about England and where he goes to school and stuff. It takes me awhile to answer all of their questions. For one thing, I have to keep my facts straight. When you're making stuff up, you've got to be careful you don't tell one person one thing and another person something different.

The most exciting message is from Megan. She asks James about his past and living in the UK. I take extra care with this one. I even include the odd English word. Like, instead of writing "French fries," I write "chips," because that's what they say over there. I end the note with James saying he must go off and watch "football" on TV, or, "as you Canadians call it, soccer."

Naturally, James mentions his pal Danny McBride. James says Danny is one of his "dearest" friends. I figure an English guy would talk like that. Why not pump myself up in Megan's eyes? Can't hurt, right?

After supper, I should be hitting the books. But I'm too wound up to do homework. Instead, I hop on the bus and go to the mall. I buy a hoodie, a cool-looking gray one that's all blinged out with metal studs.

It's the sort of store I would not have gone into before. The salesclerks look like fashion models, so you think you have to be cool to set foot in there. But now I'm more confident somehow. I walk right in.

Back home, I stand in front of the mirror, admiring myself in the new hoodie.

Just as I'm doing this rapper pose—hands crossed in front on my waist, with the hood pulled low over my eyes—Brad walks in.

"Hey, Danny," he says. "Thought I'd drop by. What's up?"

"Oh wow. You scared me," I say.

I'm kind of embarrassed that Brad saw me posing like this. He's grinning.

"Nice hoodie," is all he says. "Where'd you get it?"

"At the mall. Just bought it, like, an hour ago."

"Nice," he says.

We talk for a while. Brad tells me again that I should ask his basketball coach about being manager of the team. I'm not so sure, but I tell him again that I'll think about it.

Then Brad asks about James. He friended James today. Brad is super curious. He asks how many years I've known James and how I first met him.

And why I never mentioned James before.

Brad isn't trying to be weird or mean or anything. He's not like that. He's honestly interested. But all these questions are making me nervous.

The real clincher, though, is when Brad asks, "Do you think I could meet James sometime? He sounds like a cool guy."

"Sure. No problem," I say.

"Does he ever get over to Victoria?" Brad asks.

"Yep. Sure, he does."

"Maybe the next time, we can hang out. Like, the three of us."

"Totally, totally," I say. "Maybe he'll bring the Jag. It's British racing green, you know."

After Brad leaves, I feel almost panicky. Maybe he'll bring the Jag? It's British racing green? I must be nuts. What have I gotten myself into?

# Chapter Six

Have you ever done something you think is a good idea, and then the next day it seems like a really stupid idea?

This morning when I put it on, the hoodie I bought, it looks, well, kind of ridiculous. All these metal studs, I mean, who do I think I am? Some kind of gangster?

But when I try it on again after breakfast, it seems cool to me again. Should I wear it? Brad thought it was all right. But maybe he was just being nice. That's Brad all over. He's always super nice to everyone.

There's no time to fuss though. I throw on the hoodie and grab my backpack of books—which I didn't even open last night—and head out the door.

"What's that you're wearing?" says Mom.

"Sorry, Mom. Late for school. See ya."

School is good again, like yesterday. More kids want to know about James. It's like, because I know James, and because he's cool, maybe I'm cool too. Everyone's checking out my new hoodie too. One guy asks where I got it. I tell him, then say, "Yeah, James bought it for me." Crazy. That one just came out of me. I don't know why.

Grant, that guy on Brad's basketball team that I don't like, walks up. He's not really saying anything, but he looks me up and down with this funny expression on his face, sizing me up.

Then Grant says, "Another guy bought you clothes? Man, that's weird."

"What?" I say.

"Guys don't buy each other clothes. Are you two dating or something?"

My face is getting red. I can feel it in my cheeks.

"No, it's cool," I say. "James is from England, and it's sort of, well, an English thing. Those guys do it all the time."

By now half a dozen people have gathered around. Grant has got this look on his face that's like, "Yeah, right. Tell me another." So I cut out real quick, like I'm late for class, even though the bell won't ring for another ten minutes.

After my first class, I see Megan in the hall. I spot her from about fifteen feet away. She's wearing a dress. Or do you call it a skirt? I always forget which is which. Anyway, she looks great.

"Hi," I say.

"Hi," says Megan. "Great top. I mean, great hoodie. Looks really cool."

"Oh yeah," I say. "Thanks."

Of course, I'm tongue-tied. But in my mind, I'm starting to form a plan.

I'm going to ask Megan if she wants to have lunch with me.

It's not that big a deal, I guess. We have had lunch before. You know, me, Brad and Megan. But this is different. I'm going to ask just her. So it's like, well, a date. We'll be in the lunchroom, so it's not a big date. But it's a date all the same.

I say, "So, what are you up to today?"

"The usual. Going to classes," says Megan. "You know."

Okay, that was a stupid question to lead with. Of course Megan is going to classes. That's what we're here for. I think to myself, Danny McBride, just come out with it. Just say it.

"Yeah, classes. Right. Hey, Meg—I mean, hey, Megan. Wait, do you like Meg or Megan better?"

"Either is good," she says. "Meg. Megan."

She smiles a funny little smile that goes up higher on one side than the other. My face better not be getting red again. I wish there was a cure for that.

"Uh, okay," I say. "So you want to have lunch today?"

"Lunch? Sure. Lunchroom at noon? Or ten after, or something?"

"Um. Yeah."

"See you then."

She smiles again, turns around and walks down the hall, her backpack bouncing up and down. Wow. I can't believe it. I feel like I've won the lottery or something.

At 12:05 I run into the boys' bathroom to check myself out. I want to make sure my hair's okay. Of course, it's sticking up in a really crazy kind of way. I've noticed that whenever I look at myself in a public mirror, I look like a total dork. I grab a paper towel, wet it and push down those stupid, sticking-up hairs. There. Better.

Then I dash over to the lunchroom. Megan is sitting by herself in a corner. I walk over and sit down.

"Well, hello," I say. That was supposed to come out all cool and James Bond-like. You know, in a low voice like a movie star's. But instead it comes out in a croak. Danny the frog.

"Hi, Danny," says Megan. She doesn't seem to notice the weird voice.

We talk about school. Megan is still having trouble in math. Building up my courage, I ask if she'd like me to help her sometime. She says yes. Wow. That makes me feel great. This day is turning out pretty good, that's for sure.

I think about helping Megan with her math. For some reason, in my mind I am wearing a college professor's tweed jacket. I've got a pipe, and I'm using it to point to a blackboard that's covered with numbers.

"So, how's your friend James doing?" Megan says after awhile.

"James. Right. Well, he's doing all right. Just getting to know Canada. So different from England, you know."

Brad comes by. He pulls up a chair and plunks down his lunch bag. To be honest, I'm a little choked, because I'm finally here alone with Megan.

"Megan. Danny. Danny. Megan," says Brad, all serious-like. Then we all laugh.

We keep talking about James. Brad says I've promised that we can hang out.

Megan asks if she can come too. Of course, I say. Yes. I mean, what am I supposed to say? But all the while, I'm getting this uncomfortable feeling.

The bell rings. It's time for class, which in my case is social studies. We are studying ancient Egypt. I like listening to Mrs. Walker go on about mummies and King Tut and pyramids. One day I'd like to go to Egypt. Then again, I'd like to go anywhere. The farthest I've ever been out of Victoria is Seattle, which isn't that far.

All afternoon, I'm feeling good because I had that date with Megan. Cool, right? That's a first for me. I've gone from being Danny "No Dates" McBride to Danny "Mr. Dating Guy" McBride. Ha.

Walking home, I think over what we talked about at lunch. We talked about how we are all going to hang out with James. Then all the good feelings start to evaporate. What have I gotten myself into? How can Brad and Meg possibly meet James?

Is there a way out of this? I start to think over the possibilities, walking slower and slower, sometimes kicking a stone into the ditch. I figure if I can hatch a good plan by the time I get home, everything will be okay.

Could I convince someone to pretend to be James? It would have to be someone Meg and Brad don't know. He would have to be English or be able to talk like an English guy. And, of course, he'd have to look like the handsome dude in the FaceSpace photo. God. That is impossible.

Back home in my bedroom, I check myself out in the mirror. I remember that the kids at school said my new hoodie was cool. At least, a couple of them did. But I don't feel good about that now. This James thing is out of hand, I think. The whole deal is going to fall apart. It's going to blow up in my face like a great big...I don't know what. A big balloon filled with green paint. Guess who's going to get that green paint splashed all over his face? Me.

What am I going to do?

I do one more thing before turning in. I fire up the computer, log on as James and then have James ask Meg what she thinks of Danny McBride.

# Chapter Seven

On Saturday morning, I groan and open my right eye to look at the clock beside my bed. It's 9:02 AM. That's weird. I usually sleep until ten on the weekends.

What's that splashy sound? I open both eyes. Someone is taking a great big whiz with the bathroom door wide open. Scott. That's what woke me up. What a pig.

Scott walks out. He raises his hand to his head and then groans softly. He's wearing a *Super Troopers* T-shirt and tighty whiteys. He scratches his butt. Ugh. What a sight.

"Hey, little bro," he says, his voice all croaky. And he lights up a cigarette.

"That's gonna kill you," I say.

"What?"

"Cigarettes. Idiot."

I grab my pillow and throw it at him. It turns out to be an amazingly good shot. The pillow neatly knocks Scott's cigarette right out of his hand. It goes shooting across the room. Scott has to run over and grab the cigarette before it burns down the house or some crazy thing.

"Danny. Are you nuts?"

"No smoking. Mom says."

"Yeah. And do you do everything Mom says?"

"No," I say.

"Sure, you do. A good little Lego-making boy like you."

Suddenly, Scott jumps onto my bed and gets me in a headlock. He's laughing. And then he starts rubbing his other hand over my face and on my hair. I remember he just took a whiz and probably didn't wash his hands. So I get mad and pound Scott really hard on his back with my fist.

This takes him by surprise, I guess. He lets go and sits on the side of the bed, gasping.

"Danny. Jesus. You knocked the air right out of me."

"You asked for it. It's all that smoking. Your lungs are probably fried."

Scott starts telling me a long story about this stupid party he went to last night. The thing about my brother is, when he tells you a story, he has to tell you every detail. Like who said what to who, and what the other person said about that. It's totally boring, although you'd never know it to look at Scott. He's laughing at the funny parts and frowning at the dramatic parts.

He's talking about some guy called Chubs who ate four cheeseburgers in a row. He is telling me about Chubs trying to decide whether to order another burger or maybe a chocolate milkshake when I decide that I want to talk to Scott about James and FaceSpace. This gives me a funny feeling, like I'm about to make a presentation in front of the class.

"Um, Scott."

"Yeah?"

Scott looks up. I can't believe I'm going to tell him my big secret.

But I go ahead. Scott listens to the whole story. For once, he doesn't interrupt or make a dumb comment. Afterward, he asks to see James's profile on FaceSpace. So I show him.

Scott scrolls through it for a while. He sits back in his chair. And he lets out a long, low whistle.

"Oh man," he says. "Oh man, oh man."

This doesn't make me feel better.

"Danny. Danny McBride. Earth to Dan-o. What have you done?"

"I dunno," I say. "It's not that big a deal."

"Not that big a deal? You've invented a fake English guy. You've fooled all your friends into thinking he's a real person. And half the school knows too."

When Scott puts it that way, I start to feel a little scared.

"You know what this comes from? This comes from spending too much time at the computer. That and farting around with your Lego all the time. I think you must be going a little cuckoo," Scott says.

Ordinarily, I'd have slugged Scott in the head for saying that. But it's like all the air is sucked right out of me.

"What should I do?" I ask.

Scott sits in the computer chair, rubbing his stubbly chin. He wonders out loud whether he could pretend to be James. You know, to fool people. But that wouldn't work because, of course, Brad has known Scott as long as he's known me. Plus Scott doesn't look anything like the picture.

Then Scott wonders if he could get one of his college friends to pretend to be James. Like Chubs, maybe. Sure. Chubs is way fatter than James looks in his picture. They don't call him Chubs for nothing. But, says Scott, we could pretend that James put on a whole bunch of weight.

My brother is hatching all these ideas one after another. None of this is making me feel better. Even if we could convince this Chubs guy to go along with the scheme, there's no doubt that he would break out laughing or something in the middle of it. And then who would end up looking like a total idiot? That would be me.

Scott leaves eventually, and we haven't come up with a plan that could work. After he's gone, I sit on my bed, staring into space. Then I remember I made James ask Meg what she thinks about Danny. I mean, what she thinks about me. So I fire up the computer again. And, let me see, yes! There's a reply.

*Hi, James*, writes Meg. *Danny? He's a great guy. A little quiet at first but nice once you get to know him.*

Meg has actually written a long paragraph about me.

*I remember my first real conversation with Danny. I ran into him at a record store. He went on and on about some band I'd never heard of. But when you get to know him, Danny is a totally nice guy. He's funny. And quite good-looking.*

Did I read that right? Quite good-looking?

I jump off the chair and start doing a dance all around the bedroom. It's this funny dance I do when something really good happens to me. I call it the Apache Dance. My knees go up really high, but I barely move my arms. It's super energetic. Needless to say, I only do the Apache Dance in private, because it probably looks mental. I let out a few whoops.

From upstairs, Mom calls out, "Danny! Breakfast!" But I don't answer right away. Instead, pretending to be James, I write a reply to Meg's note about me.

*Dear Meg, You're quite right about Danny. He is a tremendous person. In fact, he's one of the best friends I've ever had.*

I drum my fingers on my desk as I try to think of more good things to say about me.

*You are indeed right about his sense of humor. He's one of the funniest guys. Also, Danny is super, super smart. I don't know any geniuses. But I think Danny is about as close to one as I've encountered.*

Hmm. What else?

*Oh yes,* I write. *Danny is also quite a party monster. Loves, loves, loves to party. It's hard to keep up with him.*

I hit *Send*, and guess what? Meg is online, and she responds right away.

*Party monster? I didn't have Danny pegged as that. He seems more the thoughtful type.*

What the heck? Who does Meg think I am? Some kind of nerd?

*No, no*, I write back. *Danny spends several nights a week partying. In fact, it surprises me that he does so well at school. He's what we in England call a party-basher.*

There. *Send.*

Meg asks James more questions. About what life was like in Britain. About how he's liking Canada. As I get caught up in the conversation, I imagine myself as James and what it would be like in a new country. Still in James mode, I tell Meg she seems good- looking from her photo. Only I write "quite striking" instead of good-looking, as that seems more English.

*James, do you ever visit Victoria?* Meg writes.

*Yes, quite often. I'll be there tomorrow, in fact,* I write.

*How about meeting for coffee, or hot chocolate? Or tea? 'Cause you're British. LOL!*

*Yes, that would be lovely.*

*Okay. Why don't we say 2:00 pm? There's a coffee shop across from our school*, writes Meg. *It's a date.* She adds a smiley face.

*I look forward to it, my dear. See you then.* I write as James. I figure James would say something like "my dear."

Then, just when I'm feeling all good about setting up a date with Meg, Scott walks back in.

"I thought you were going out," I say.

"I did. I'm back. Hey, do you have that James FaceSpace page on your computer?"

When Scott says that, it brings me back to reality. It's not me who just made a date with Meg. It's James. And it's tomorrow! What. Was. I. Thinking.

I've already told Scott about the whole fake James thing. So I tell him what just happened.

"Danny. Jeez. I can't believe you did that. You're not making things better, you know. We already agreed we don't know anyone who could pretend to be James. Unless you want Chubs."

"No, I do not want Chubs. I already told you that wouldn't work."

I groan, jump on my bed and stuff my head under the pillow. Why did I arrange for James to meet Meg? Mom calls me to breakfast again, only way louder this time. So I go upstairs, but not before telling Scott to keep a lid on my secret.

It's hard to enjoy myself, even though it's Saturday. I meet up with Brad. We shoot hoops at the outdoor court at the school, then hang out at the mall for a couple of hours. It's fun. We buy hot dogs at Orange Julius and talk to some kids from school. It's the sort of stuff I like doing.

At the same time, in the back of my mind, I'm thinking about Meg. It's like a black cloud. Every time Brad says something funny and I laugh, I also think about this stupid date.

On the other hand, Meg did say some nice things about me. So it's not all bad, right? Man, I don't know. This situation is getting out of hand.

# Chapter Eight

On Sunday morning I wake up even earlier than I did on Saturday. All night I had strange dreams about being chased down the hallways of an old-fashioned mansion.

In the dream, something's after me, but I can't see who or what it is. That makes it even worse. Just before I wake up, the evil thing finally catches up to me, and its icy hands surround my body.

It feels like a ghost breathing on me. Only I'm being grabbed somehow.

I open my eyes, all groggy and confused. Then I sit bolt upright. Uh-oh. Today's the day. Today James is going to meet Meg. The question is, how?

There's only one solution. James has to die. That's the only way out of this. If something happens to James—like he's in a car accident—then he can't visit Victoria and Meg. Obviously, being dead and all.

"James must die, James must die," I think to myself. I get up and start pulling on my clothes. Then Scott stirs in the other bed.

"Danny. What are you talking about? You woke me up."

"What do you mean?"

"All this 'James must die stuff.' What's up with that?"

Yikes. I must have started saying it aloud. Am I losing my mind or what?

When Scott goes upstairs for breakfast, I put on some Black Sabbath. It's an old song called "Paranoid." Early heavy metal, from the seventies, with driving guitar. The singer sounds like some crazy guy on a hilltop cradling a machine gun.

"Paranoid" goes like this: *People think I'm insane because I am frowning all the time/All day long I think of things but nothing seems to satisfy.*

Mom yells at me to turn down the music and come up for breakfast. I snap out of it. The weird thing is, I've dressed myself all in black without realizing it. I'm wearing a black T-shirt, black jeans and black jacket, even. I check myself out in the mirror. I look like one of those crazy goth teenagers who go on murderous rampages. My face is all angry-looking, like the guy's in the Black Sabbath song.

I've got to pull myself together.

The morning goes by too quickly. It's almost noon before I know it.

Two more hours before Meg meets James. What to do?

I log in as James on FaceSpace. There are tons of new friend requests for him. There are no new messages though. Almost without thinking, I type a status update for James.

*Ran into some tough-looking dudes today. One guy looked like a gangster. Scary-looking.*

A couple of people comment with stuff like, *Really?* and *Tell us more.* I think for a second, then write,

*We live in a mixed neighborhood, close to East Van. You see a lot of crackle-heads.*

I should have said crackheads, but I was typing too fast. Of course, right away a bunch of guys make fun of that. Saying stuff like, *Crackle-heads? Dude, do you even know what you're talking about?*

Bad mistake. James is supposed to be cool.

*We called them crackle-heads in the UK,* I write quickly. No one questions it. I dodged a bullet there.

Meanwhile, I'm thinking about a plan. Let's say James runs into some bad guys in Vancouver. Drug dealers or something like that. There's a gunfight, and James gets caught in the cross fire. A hail of bullets. Yeah.

The more I think about this idea, the more excited I get. I realize I can create a really cool memorial page for James, an amazing tribute made by his very best pal, Danny McBride. I can make it elaborate, with pictures of where he used to live in Britain and all that. It'll be fun. And everyone will think I'm a good guy for doing it. "What a super nice person Danny is," they'll think.

Admittedly, there are a few holes in my plan. For one thing, some kids might want to know if James is going to have an actual memorial service.

They might want to go. That's a detail that could be worked out, I guess.

This isn't going to solve the problem of James meeting up with Meg today. It is 12:47 already. James is supposed to be at the coffee shop in an hour. If only I'd thought of this gangster thing before. If only I hadn't let my imagination get away with me.

The funny thing is, I know I'm not going to cancel the coffee date. It's sort of like if James has a date with Meg, then I do too. Know what I mean? James is my creation, after all.

James is me.

At 1:45, I head out the door. I've traded my goth, psycho-killer outfit for something a little less intense. I'm wearing jeans and a green tennis shirt. My plan? I'm not sure yet.

The coffee shop is across from the school. It's one of those places with big windows. You can see right in.

As I get closer, I see Meg sitting there, bent over. It looks like she's texting or something.

Oh man. What to do? Usually, I can come up with something, but today I'm drawing a blank. There's a row of bushes by the coffee shop. I creep up behind them. Just to get a closer peek.

There's this big branch in my way, blocking the view. When I move to try and get a better view, my foot hits something slippery. I tumble forward, and I roll out of the bushes. My right leg clunks against the window of the coffee shop. Right in front of Meg. Makes this huge *clong* that has everyone in the shop looking in my direction.

Meg looks up right away. She's startled—she's got that deer-in-the-headlights look. Then she smiles and waves.

What can I do? Of course, I go in to say hi.

"Hey, Meg."

"Danny. What's up?"

"Oh, you know. Not much. Just going for a walk, like."

"Were you hiding in the bushes?" says Meg.

"What bushes?"

"The bushes you fell out of a minute ago."

"Oh yeah," I say. "Well, I was just checking those bushes out. Because, um, because Mom wants to get new bushes to go in front of the house. And these look like really good ones. Really thick leaves, you know."

Meg smiles. She can tell my story is bogus. But she's too nice to say so. That makes me feel even worse.

"Anyway, Meg. I'm also here for another reason."

"Really? What?"

"James sent me here." I'm making this up as I go along.

"He did?" says Meg. She frowns.

"Uh, yeah. James is worried that he's being followed. That, like, someone is after him."

Then I tell her this story about how James lives in a bad part of Vancouver. I tell her that he ran into some tough guys and, through no fault of his own, got into a hassle with them. I tell Meg there was some misunderstanding, that these bad guys have mistaken James for someone else. I tell her they chased him down the street and yelled that they were gonna get him. I finish by saying that it's curtains for James.

"Curtains?" says Meg. "What do you mean?"

Why did I say "curtains"? That's so lame. I must have got that from an old gangster movie or something.

"I think it's an English term, curtains. Anyway, James wanted to be here, but he didn't think it was safe to travel. He's going to lay low for a few days. He's really, really sorry."

Meg looks disappointed. And puzzled. She tells me to sit down, since I'm there, and have a hot chocolate with her. Her treat. Hey, this is working out good.

"Danny," says Meg after awhile. "James tells me you're quite the party guy."

"What?" I say.

"Yeah, he told me on FaceSpace. That you party a couple of times a week."

I take a long, slow drink of my hot chocolate. It gives me time to think.

"Yes," I finally say. "I do like to party. Quite a bit. Partying is excellent."

"I've never seen you at any of the parties the kids at school have," says Meg.

"Yes," I say. "Well, that's because I like to go to parties with older kids. You know. Grade eleven, grade twelve.

Those guys are more…mature, like. We have more in-depth conversations."

"Really?" Meg smiles. What is she thinking?

Then she invites me to a party she's having that night. She's going to invite Brad too. It's a last-minute thing. It won't be a big party, she says, just a few friends. Close friends.

"If James changes his mind about coming to Victoria, tell him to come too," says Meg. "I have a feeling if you're there, he might want to come."

She smiles again, like she has a secret.

I watch Meg leave the coffee shop. Outside, she waves and then walks down the street. With my spoon, I scoop out the chunky stuff from the bottom of my cup of hot chocolate. I'm feeling pretty happy. I'm invited to a party. And oh yeah, Meg said it was for her close friends. I must be one of them!

What did she mean about James coming though? I think through my story again. Meg didn't say much about it. Does she know the whole James thing is a big fat lie?

# Chapter Nine

Later that day, Brad phones. He wants us to go to Meg's party together. And he asks if I want to stay over, because his house is three blocks from Meg's place.

The added bonus is that if we stay late, my mom won't know. She's pretty strict about staying out late on school nights.

Adrian Chamberlain

Before Brad joined the basketball team, we had lots of sleepovers.
We'd watch scary movies or play Risk.
Brad's mom would make us these huge
bowls of popcorn.

So this will be like the good old
days. I'm pretty psyched about it.

For the rest of the afternoon, I work
on Lego City. I'm building an overpass
over the city. It's supposed to be like a
rapid-transit system. Like an overhead
subway. That way, people can leave
their cars at home, avoid traffic jams
and get to work a lot faster. And if they
do this, it will cause less pollution.

Working on Lego City takes my mind
off any worries I might have. I don't
think about the James situation or the
homework that is piling up again.

Mom notices at dinner that I'm
different. That's because I don't eat
much, even though she's made a whole
mess of homemade French fries. I don't

say much either. I'm a little uptight about the party. It's gonna be fun and all. But I can be shy around new people.

Mom asks if I'm feeling well and wonders if I should stay at home. In case I'm catching the flu or something. I start scarfing down the fries on my plate. Mom can be overprotective sometimes.

After supper, I get ready for the party. I put on my fancy hoodie. I'm checking myself out in the mirror, trying to get my stupid hair to stop sticking up, when Brad walks into the bedroom.

"Hey, boy-o," he says, punching my arm.

Scott gives us a ride. His sports car has only two seats, which means Brad and I have to share the passenger seat. It looks sort of weird. Too close for comfort, right? But we joke around and laugh it off.

Megan's house is real nice. It's colonial style, with brick columns.

It looks like a Monopoly house come to life. Her folks must be rich. Inside, it's decorated for the party with balloons. There are good snacks too. It's not just chips and dip. It's special stuff— crackers and shrimp, like you'd have at a party for adults.

"Hi, Brad. Hi, Danny. Where's James?" says Megan. She smiles. Brad raises one eyebrow really high, like some goofball from a TV sitcom. Everyone laughs. Me too, even though I'm wishing this whole James thing would just go away.

It turns out that I know a bunch of people here. Most, I recognize from school. We sit around listening to tunes. Then someone starts a trivia game where you try to guess who was in what movie, or who sang what song. It's awesome.

After the game, we talk about our hobbies. Some girl says she takes

FaceSpace

riding lessons. A guy says he and his dad are restoring a 1936 Chevy. Not making a hot rod but doing it stock, like bringing it back to new.

When it comes to my turn, I start talking about the architectural design I do on my computer. The kids at the party are actually saying, "Hey, cool" and, "Wow." I feel all encouraged and excited, so I start talking about Lego City.

Then Grant says, "Oh man, McBride. You don't mean you still play with Lego."

"What do you mean?" I say.

"Only little kids play with Lego. You must be a total dork."

You know how when something really bad happens, time slows down? That's what happens to me. All the kids look at me. I feel my face getting hot.

So I say, "Hey, Grant, I'm talking about Lego City the *band*."

"What?" says Grant.

"I'm talking about Lego City the band. They're, like, underground rock. You've probably never even heard of them."

Grant's smile disappears.

"You're making that up, McBride."

Brad looks at me funny for a second. Then he says, "Yeah, Grant. You've never heard of Lego City? They rock, dude."

All the kids look like they expect something to happen. Grant looks choked, like he wants to take a swing at me. So I do something, well, kind of weird.

I say, "This is Lego City's greatest hit." And then I start making up this crazy song. The words are like, *If you wanna get to Lego City/You gotta get down and sing this ditty…* Stuff like that. I stand up and start doing a spazzy dance.

What's gotten into me? This could be a really bad move. But then Meg gets up and starts dancing with me. And then everyone else starts dancing too. Well, everyone but Grant.

I don't know why, but all of this makes me feel really good. I'm thinking, hey, just be yourself, people will be okay with that. Even if your real self is goofy.

The party is really great. I don't know when I've had such a good time. By the time Brad and I say goodbye to everyone, it's about midnight.

The only downer is, it turns out Grant is staying at Brad's too. His folks are away, so they asked if Grant could sleep over. I don't like that. For one thing, Grant still seems choked at me over the Lego City thing. Walking to Brad's, he doesn't talk to me. In fact, he doesn't say much. Brad and I talk up a storm though.

We all sleep in this room Brad says is his dad's "man cave." It's got a giant flat-screen TV, a great surround-sound system and a fancy computer. We all have sleeping bags. It's kind of like camping.

Grant falls asleep in thirty seconds. Brad and I keep talking, but quietly, so we won't wake up anyone.

Then Brad falls asleep too. I sit up and look at the clock. It's after one o'clock, but I can't sleep yet. I'm too revved up.

I tiptoe over to the computer and turn it on. The light is bright, so I turn it down to low. Then I log on to James's profile page on FaceSpace. I write a new status update.

*Guys, I'm really scared. Those gangster guys? They're following me. I don't know what's going on but am expecting the worst.*

Hmm. Does that sound fake? I don't know. I start a brand-new FaceSpace page. It's a memorial page for James. I figure I'll begin working on it now, for when the bad guys have killed James. But after fifteen minutes, I'm so sleepy that I just slip into my sleeping bag and close my eyes.

# Chapter Ten

I wake up hot and groggy. This isn't my room. Then I remember that I slept at Brad's place. We went to a party. And it's Monday morning. I have school.

I have a pounding headache too. I hear whispering.

I poke my head out of the sleeping bag. Brad and Grant are in front of the computer. They almost sound like they're having an argument. A real quiet one though.

Uh-oh. Did I log off the computer last night?

Brad looks over his shoulder and catches my eye.

"Hey, Danny," he says. He sounds strange.

Grant turns around. He's grinning this big, fat, stupid grin.

"McBride. We were just looking at your memorial page for James. You know, the fake English dude you made up on FaceSpace." He laughs this really harsh-sounding laugh. And then he kicks me right through the sleeping bag.

"You faked this whole thing, McBride! What a loser," he says.

"Shut up, Grant," says Brad. "You're gonna wake my folks."

I'm getting this sinking feeling, like the whole world is collapsing. I get out of the sleeping bag and stand up, trying to see the computer screen.

"What are you talking about, Grant?" I say, stalling for time.

"What am I talking about? I'm talking about how you signed yourself in as James and started to write about gangsters. And now you're making a memorial page for him? That is so friggin' weird, McBride. You must be crazy," he says.

I deny everything. I mean, what am I gonna do? I'm not going to come clean in front of Grant, that's for sure. It's a relief when he leaves to do his paper route before school.

After he goes, Brad looks at me.

"What?" I say.

"Danny," he says. "Come on."

I tell Brad everything. How I made up James. How I got fake photos of him and his family's Jaguar. How I

Photoshopped him and me into the same photograph.

"Why'd you do all that, Danny?" says Brad.

"I dunno. I guess—oh man. I figured knowing James would make me popular. He's cool, so maybe that would make me cool too."

Brad sits on a chair and lets out a low whistle. He rubs his face and looks at me again.

"You know Grant will tell everyone at school about this," he says.

"Yeah," I say. "I'm doomed. I'm toast. My life as I know it is basically over."

Brad smiles for the first time.

"Hey, it's not that bad."

I feel like getting back in that sleeping bag and never getting out again. Maybe I'll go into hibernation for the rest of my life. What will the kids at school think? What will Meg think? She's going to hate me. I know it.

"It just seemed like everyone on FaceSpace was having more fun than me," I finally say.

"What do you mean?"

"Well, take you. You have, like, five million friends. And you're always doing cool stuff. Parties, hanging out with people," I say. "I never go to parties. That one last night at Meg's? That's the first proper party I ever went to."

Brad blinks twice. So I go on.

"You and I used to hang out all the time. Now you're always busy with your basketball buddies."

It makes me feel weird to say this. Guys aren't supposed to talk like this, right?

"Hey, Danny. Bud. You've got it all wrong," says Brad.

"What do you mean?" I say.

"My life is pretty much the same as yours. I go to school. I'm trying to keep up in my classes. And I'm having trouble.

I haven't got a clue what's going on in math. I'm probably gonna fail. I haven't even told Mom and Dad yet."

That surprises me. Brad was always good at school. He was always good at everything.

"I'm not going to parties all the time. Maybe the odd one. But it's not like it looks on FaceSpace. Everyone always posts updates that make it look like they're having a great time. That's not the truth. It isn't for me anyway."

"Well," I say, wiping my face with my sleeve. "You're partying way more than me."

"I only go to parties because I'm on the team. If you were on the team, you'd be part of that."

"Yeah. Well, I'm no good in sports. That's the problem," I say.

"Danny. Man, there's all kinds of things you could join. You're a smart guy. You're funny. You're a cool dude.

A crazy dude, but still cool," Brad says. He punches me on the shoulder.

"I'm cool. Yeah, right."

"No man, you are. Hey, you're my best friend. I wouldn't have a knob for a best friend."

"I thought Grant was your best friend."

"Grant? Don't make me laugh," says Brad.

"Why do you hang out with him then? Why did he stay over last night?"

"My folks made me. Grant's going through a tough time right now. His parents are divorcing. His mom doesn't want him, so he's going to move with his dad to Vancouver. And, between you and me, I don't think his dad wants him either."

I know that in a few hours Grant will tell the whole school the truth about James. But, to tell the truth, I actually feel a little sorry for Grant right now.

"Maybe I should invent a new person on FaceSpace," I say. "Someone who could tell everyone that James is a real guy. Maybe that's the way—"

"Danny," says Brad. "Come on, buddy."

"Yeah. Dumb idea."

"You're going to have to face it. It won't be so bad."

Brad punches me in the arm again. It's funny. I feel both terrible and good at the same time.

"Megan's gonna think I'm a total jerk," I say.

"Well, she's probably not going to be thrilled. Didn't you send her to meet James for coffee?"

Brad starts to laugh. It's not really funny. In fact, it's downright sad. But, after a minute, I start to smile.

Brad and I walk to school together. We chat a mile a minute, like in the old days. The sun shines. Our feet crunch through oak leaves on the sidewalk. All the while, I have this nervous feeling. I wish I could start going to a different school. Also, I start thinking how I goofed around with Brad's photos on FaceSpace. What kind of friend am I? I'm going to change my ways.

# Chapter Eleven

Remember when you first went to school? Like, in grade one? You're all scared. You have that funny feeling in your gut, like a bunch of lizards are running around down there. That's how I feel walking through the doors of my school that morning.

It's not so bad at first. My first class is English. Mr. Kerr is going on about adverbs, and all the other kids seem as bored as I am. Then, in between classes in the halls, I start to notice it. Kids are staring. A few are laughing.

The word must be officially out. Danny McBride made up a fake friend on FaceSpace. To make himself popular. What a dork. What a knob. What a tool. At least, that's what I imagine they are saying. Argh!

At lunchtime, I see Grant and his basketball buddies in the hall near my locker. Grant is laughing, slapping one of them on the back. When he sees me, his face lights up like it's Christmas morning.

"There he is! McBride! Hey, doofus, where's your imaginary friend James? You know, that super cool dude from England?" Grant yells. His freckly face is bright red. Combined with his orange hair—which sticks out all over the place—he looks almost bonkers.

"You're making up people on FaceSpace? What a loser!" says one of Grant's friends.

"Get lost, Grant," I say, throwing my books in my locker.

"Get lost yourself, McBride. Loser, loser!"

Grant makes the sign of an *L* with his fingers, grinning like a madman. I feel like I might throw up. My face burns. My stomach gurgles. I can even hear it. Keep it together, Danny. You don't want to upchuck in the school hallway.

"Hey, Danny. Let's go to lunch, bro." Brad throws his arm around my shoulder. The crowd that has gathered starts to break up. I don't dare look up, but I hear the voices getting fainter.

"Brad, I can't believe you still hang out with McBride. That guy is so incredibly lame," says Grant.

"Hey, it was just a prank, Grant," I say. My voice sounds all thick. My mouth is dry and gritty, like someone dumped a spoonful of beach sand into it.

"Prank, my butt. You—"

"Drop it, Grant," says Brad. "Get lost."

Brad sounds firm, like a teacher you can't disobey. A look flickers over Grant's face. For a second, I think he's going to slug me. Or Brad. But finally Grant just shrugs and walks away.

"Come on, Danny," says Brad. "Let's go."

In the lunchroom, everyone is whispering about me. Or, at least, that's what I think. Two girls bend their heads toward each other, smiling. Can it get any worse?

Yes, it can. As soon as we sit down— me with a cafeteria-bought cheese sandwich and a Coke—Megan joins Brad and me. She doesn't look happy.

"So is it true?" she says right away. No hello or anything.

"What?" I say.

"That you faked James. Set me up on a coffee date with a made-up guy. Is that true?"

Megan looks mad. I've never seen her like this. Her face is all tight-looking, her mouth sort of pulled in.

"Yeah." I sigh and push my sandwich away. "It's true. I'm sorry. I'm a jerk."

And then, for the second time that day, I tell the whole story. Well, most of it. I leave out the part where I wanted to be as popular as Brad. That would make me look like a total loser—or rather, more of one.

Megan looks mad the whole time. She just asks these short questions, like a police interrogator on TV.

Brad sticks up for me whenever he can, saying stuff like, "Danny just has an overactive imagination" and, "Danny's a good guy, he just made a mistake."

"I feel like an idiot," I say finally. "I guess everyone hates me."

Megan's face finally goes back to normal. "No. That's not true," she says. "It was a pretty weird thing to do, and I'm still mad."

"I'm really sorry."

"Well, you should be. But don't feel too bad. Hey, you know, my friends really liked you at my party," says Megan.

I'd almost forgotten about the party. It seems like a thousand years ago now.

"Really?" I say.

"Oh yeah. They thought you were smart and funny. And Kelly? She said she thought you were cute."

Cute? Me? That makes me feel better. I take a bite out of my sandwich and open my Coke can with a loud *pop*. Then I take a long drink. Man, I'm thirsty. Public humiliation will do that to a guy, I guess.

As Megan leaves for her first afternoon class, she rests her hand on my shoulder for a second. Maybe I should buy her a present to say I'm sorry. What do girls like? Flowers or something. I'll ask Scott about that. He's the expert in the girl department.

Brad and I have a spare block, so we don't have to rush back to class. We talk more. Brad says maybe I should lay off the computer, stay away from FaceSpace for a week. He also says I should talk to his basketball coach. They still need a team manager, and I could probably have the job if I want it. It would be fun. I could be part of the team. I wouldn't be a player, but we could all hang out together.

I tell Brad I don't want to manage any team that Grant is on. He reminds me that Grant is moving to Vancouver. I tell Brad I'll think about it. In fact, I've got a lot to think about.

The sun is still shining when I walk home after school. Today has been rough, sure enough. But it was not as terrible as I thought it was going to be. Do you ever find that? You know, you're really dreading something. But when it actually happens, it's not so bad after all.

After supper, I log on to FaceSpace. First I delete James's profile. I feel a little sad doing this, like I've lost a friend. So long, James.

I also fix those photos of Brad so they're back to normal. There done.

Then I work on my architectural drawings for a while. I add an observatory to my fantasy house. I figure the guy who lives there will want to see all the planets and the stars. He'll probably want to imagine life in far-off galaxies.

Around eight, my mom calls out to me from upstairs.

"Danny," she says. "Want to play Parcheesi?"

Parcheesi? Argh. Welcome to the exciting life of Danny McBride.

"Okay, Mom!" I yell. I shut down the computer and run upstairs. I don't really mind playing Parcheesi if it makes Mom happy. And I sort of like it.

But let's keep that between you and me. Okay?

Adrian Chamberlain is a news-paper reporter. Like his character in *FaceSpace*, he spends most of his time trying to make sense of the world around him. He has never owned a Lego set but would like to buy one. His interests include playing music and hanging out with his pug dog, Ollie. Adrian lives in Victoria, British Columbia.

# orca currents

For more information on all the books
in the Orca Currents series, please visit
**www.orcabook.com**